AMELIARANNE
KEEPS SCHOOL

·TOLD·BY· CONSTANCE ·HEWARD·

·PICTURED· ·BY~S·B· ·PEARSE·

COLLINS
PICTURE LIONS

AMELIARANNE sat up in bed in the moonlight and rubbed her sleepy eyes. It wasn't the whisper of the soft June breeze in the ivy that had awakened her, but a strangely unusual noise. There it was again.

"*Bow-wow-wow-w-w! Wow-wow-w-w! Ow-wow-w-w!*" and, with the mournful howl, a gentle scratching at the Stigginses' front door.

"It's a dog that's got lost," Ameliaranne whispered, and she slipped noiselessly out of bed and tiptoed down the stairs in the moonlight.

When Ameliaranne opened the cottage door,
the dog came in with a bounce. He was a black
spaniel, and he licked Ameliaranne's face and
hands and her bare pink toes, while she loved
and patted him, and said,

"Ssh, ssh, good doggie!"

Then Mrs Stiggins came downstairs with a
light and said,

"Ameliaranne, whatever ———?" But her
words ended in a gasp, for the dog sat up and
begged, and Ameliaranne said,

"There's the stew that was left from dinner,"
and she ran to the pantry to fetch it.

The dog's collar showed that his name was Robin, and that he belonged to Miss Penny-winn, who kept a boarding-school on the edge of the town. Ameliaranne had seen Miss Penny-winn's nice little boys and girls out walking, and she had made up her mind to keep a boarding-school herself when she grew up.

"It's a holiday at our school tomorrow, so we can take him back," she said, joyfully, as she made a comfy bed for Robin in the old arm-chair.

When the five little Stigginses came downstairs
the next morning, they were surprised to find
a dog in the kitchen, but Robin was used to
children and he shook a paw and begged for
titbits. After breakfast Mrs Stiggins said, "Run
along, Ameliaranne, for I don't doubt but what
Miss Pennywinn will be anxious about him."

Everyone watched as Ameliaranne tied a
long string to Robin's collar. Richard and
Rosabel and Jenny and Joey didn't want to go
to Miss Pennywinn's. They wanted to play
with their new cricket bat. Wee William
thought it would be more fun to hold the string,
so he and Ameliaranne set out down the road
with Robin pulling like a frisky horse.

When they reached Miss Pennywinn's house in its big garden, Ameliaranne went in at the back gate, and she had just taken the string from Wee William, when Robin bolted towards the open kitchen door.

Ameliaranne clung to the string and Wee William clung to her, as the dog dashed through the kitchen into the hall. The school-room door was ajar, and Robin plunged into the midst of Miss Pennywinn's pupils, but Ameliaranne and Wee William sat down with two big bumps on the floor.

The children shouted, "Robin's come back! Hurrah!" and Miss Pennywinn was so glad that her dog was found, and so surprised to see two strange children sitting there, that she let them shout. And Jemima, the cook, and Judy, the housemaid, who had been making beds upstairs looked in at the door, and then Miss Pennywinn said, *"Silence, please!"* in a very loud voice. But Ameliaranne saw a twinkle in her eyes, and she jumped up, and pulled Wee William to his feet, and told the story.

Miss Pennywinn said she had heard about the Stiggins family, and she thought it most kind of them to have taken care of Robin. Then a telegram came for her, and after she had read it she said,

"Dear, dear! My sister has wired that she cannot meet the new little boy who arrives from India today, and I must go to the city at once to meet him. What can we do, Jemima? I cannot leave you and Judy with all these children."

Jemima said, "That you can't, mum. I'll cook for 'em as long as you please, but don't you ask me to mind 'em."

But Ameliaranne said, "Oh, please, Miss Pennywinn, I'm *very* used to minding children, and I'm going to keep a school when I'm grown up."

And Miss Pennywinn laughed and said that Ameliaranne could begin keeping school at once, if she was sure that Mrs Stiggins wouldn't be anxious about her and Wee William, and then she rushed away to get ready for her journey.

The schoolroom was large and Ameliaranne spied a wash-basin in one corner, with a shelf above it full of paint-boxes and mugs. Bobby Binns made room at his desk for Wee William, who just as Ameliaranne was about to begin, let out a sound that was half a shriek and half a gurgle. The children giggled, but Ameliaranne couldn't take her eyes off Wee William, who was wriggling about, his shoulders hunched up to his ears, his eyes screwed up tight and a queer, twisty sort of smile on his face. Suddenly a white mouse popped out at his neck, ran to the top of his head, and, sitting up on its hind legs, began to wash its face with its front paws.

While everyone shrieked with delight, Bobby Binns tucked Nib the mouse away in his trouser pocket. Ameliaranne told him firmly that if she caught him putting it down anyone's neck again, she would take it away from him. Then she said, "Now you can all paint a picture of Robin howling outside our cottage door in the moonlight." So paint-boxes were taken down and mugs filled, and the children were soon as busy as bees.

Ameliaranne walked about among her pupils, flourishing a paint-brush. When she found Bobby Binns and Wee William painting each other's faces to look like Red Indians, she marched them to the wash-basin and washed them with a very firm hand.

When the pictures were finished they looked beautiful, and Ameliaranne pinned them round the walls for Miss Pennywinn to see.

After that, Ameliaranne made every child clean his paint-box and wash his mug, and then somebody said, "Let's dress up!"

Now, though Ameliaranne loved dressing up, she didn't know whether she ought to allow it in school, but when she saw the costumes inside the chest against the wall, she said,

"Well, you can dress up, but you must all pretend that you're the people you look like," and then she had her hands full giving out the costumes.

One little girl was a queen, and one was a grandmother, and there were several fairies, but the funniest sight was the very fat child who dressed up as a baby. Then there was a bus-conductor, a tram-driver and a policeman. Bobby Binns chose a Red Indian's suit, and Wee William was a poor old Robinson Crusoe, with an umbrella blown inside out.

But Ameliaranne put on a tight-fitting dress, which reached down to her ankles and up to her chin and made her feel like a real school-mistress.

While the children were busy admiring one another, Judy burst into the schoolroom, her cap awry and her face and hair covered with smuts.

"There's a brick fell down the kitchen chimerny, and the dinner's spoilt," she gasped.

There was a horried smell of burning soot as Ameliaranne and the children followed Judy to the kitchen, and Jemima greeted them with,

"There'll be no dinner for any of you today, for Judy and me are smothered with soot, likewise the meat and pudding and pertaters."

Ameliaranne felt troubled that there was to be no dinner, and as she noticed two garden seats on the lawn where the children were standing, she had an idea. Pulling the seats to face each other, she said,

"This is a tram. We've got a driver and a conductor, and the others can be passengers. The policeman is on point-duty, and Robinson Crusoe has just got back from his island and he's asking the way home. I'll be back in a minute."

Ameliaranne ran to the kitchen.

"Please, Miss Jemima," she said, politely, "We don't want meat and potatoes and pudding, but can we have some bread and jam out in the garden? It would save you a lot of washing up."

And Jemima, who was really very kind, stopped washing the soot off the potatoes and said, "Well, that's common-sensible. There's everything we'll need in the larder, so we'll wash our faces and handses, and before you can say 'diddle diddle dandy' you'll be fed."

When the picnic was ready the bus-conductor shouted *"Terminus!"* and the passengers got out and sat on the lawn, but he and the driver ate their dinner in the tram, and the policeman stayed on point-duty, beckoning solemnly whenever he wanted something more to eat.

As Robinson Crusoe hadn't found his way home, he sat at the policeman's feet, and Ameliaranne kept everyone in order, and snatched a bite now and again as she handed out sandwiches and jam tarts, and sugared biscuits and ginger pop.

After the picnic Ameliaranne told the children a story, and after that they begged her to come and see the see-saw and swing and sand-pit.

Ameliaranne said, "Well, just for a minute, and then you'll have to do some more lessons."

A man was mending the swing, and Ameliaranne was delighted to see that it was Mr Jubb, the joiner, and Mr Jubb asked if it was a fancy-dress party, and said he'd have to walk wary with a real live policeman on the spot.

Mr Jubb was sucking a big toffee, and passed round a paper bag full of them. He had lots of spare nails and bits of wood too, and the boys hammered while the girls played in the sand-pit.

Then Ameliaranne suddenly remembered she was keeping school and said, *"Silence, please!"* just as Miss Pennywinn had done, but before she could tell them to march back to the schoolroom, Bobby Binns wailed out, "I've lost my mouse!"

Nib had enjoyed the picnic, and the bus-conductor was sure that he had put him into his bag again after the meal was over. Nib wasn't there now, however, and Bobby Binns said hopefully, "Robin will find him!"

But Robin had also disappeared, and Mr Jubb, who had mended the swing and collected his tools, slung his bag onto his back, and went away, promising to call and tell Mrs Stiggins that Ameliaranne was keeping school.

Robin came back soon from burying a bone, and the children went on searching the rambling old garden till they came to a most untidy plot of ground, and there they all exclaimed,

"Why, it's Monday, and it's gardening!" And Bobby Binns forgot his mouse and said,

"You see, we couldn't garden last week because it rained, and Miss Pennywinn said we'd got to pull out every weed this afternoon."

Ameliaranne's eyes sparkled as she led her
pupils back to the schoolroom. Her Uncle Joe
was a gardener, and he had taught her a lot of
things. She soon had the children back in their
everyday clothes and the fancy dresses folded
neatly away in the chest, and then they all put
on their overalls and fetched their tools from
the tool-shed, and they hoed and raked and
chattered and kept Ameliaranne very busy
indeed.

They grew whatever they liked and each garden was separated from the next by a narrow, pebbled path. Ameliaranne found dusky-faced pansies and sweet-smelling pinks, and bachelors' buttons, clumps of budding cornflowers and poppies. One little garden was a potato patch, and another just had radishes and mustard and cress. There were feathery-topped carrots and bunchy-topped turnips, and, when the children had finished, the plot looked as neat as a dolls-house garden.

But Bobby Binns was sad because of his lost pet, and after they had put away their tools, they hunted for Nib again.

Just then Judy came out to say that tea was ready, and they all marched back to the schoolroom, washed their hands and sat down at the table. Just then a taxi arrived, and out stepped Miss Pennywinn and the boy from India.

Miss Pennywinn put him beside Ameliaranne. But Ameliaranne looked out of the window and said, "Oh, please Miss Pennywinn, there's Mother with the little ones," and Miss Pennywinn sent Judy to bring the Stigginses in.

Mrs Stiggins said she'd brought what Mr Jubb took home in his tool-bag, and gave Miss Pennywinn a box, and when the box was opened, Bobby Binns shouted joyfully, "It's Nib! It's Nib!"

Miss Pennywinn made Bobby put Nib into his cage, and then Judy set places for the little Stigginses, and Mrs Stiggins went to have tea in the kitchen.

Miss Pennywinn's eyes twinkled when she heard about the brick, and the dressing up and the picnic, and, when she saw the gardens after tea, she was delighted, and she thanked Ameliaranne very much indeed for keeping school.

Then the Stigginses said goodbye, and Ameliaranne whispered to Robin that she'd be sure to bring him back whenever he liked to get lost.

proost Turnhout (Belgium)

PRINTED IN BELGIUM